Life and It's Depression

Written By Annastasia

D1528456

THE FOLLOWING STORY IS A FICTIONAL (IMAGINARY) STORY

The setting is a real place and some of the names in this story are real people but are not based on true events. The story's purpose is for the reader to overcome their struggles and their mind that is working against them.

DEDICATED TO ALL JOB CORP STUDENTS (SPECIFICALLY DETROIT JOB CORP)

SHOUT OUT TO MS. FLOOD-EDWARDS, MR. MOORE, MR. SINGAL, MS. LEROY, MR. ATTIEH, MR. BROWN, MS. STEPHENS, MR. CLEAVES, AND MS. RANONI.

IMPORTANT TOPICS

Addiction

Anxiety

Believing in Yourself

Bullying

Death

Depression

Drugs

Failure

Mental Illness

Self Worth

Success

Happiness.

TABLE OF CONTENTS

Chapter One
DEPRESSION

DEPRESSION. Just utter depression.

Why do I even exist? I'll tell you why. Because two idiots with no money, no support and not even all there mentally decided "hey, let's have a baby." Practically half of America has that mindset. Now look where I'm at. A teacher yelled at me because I got an 'F.' Okay, maybe it was more than one 'F'.

"A 'F' again, Amara?"

I thought life was pointless. There was nothing for me. No family, no support. No one to give me congratulations or to tell me that they loved me. Only people to tell me that I was a failure surrounded me. I didn't like myself. They say your first love is supposed to be yourself So, why don't you like me?

Loving yourself is the first step to enjoying life. That was part of the problem. I didn't enjoy life because I didn't like myself. I'm different though. I'm self-aware of my failures. I know that I am one. I know that I am someone that will eventually become nothing. So, what's the point?

I gave my teacher Mr. Martin a death glare. This was the third time this week that he had pulled me out of class to talk to me about my work.

It was infuriating to know that people expected something better out of me. An F is all I'm worth. Why couldn't he just accept that? Why couldn't everybody just accept that I'm not worth saving?

I stay silent and he continues with his lecture. "Seriously, Amara. This is your fifth F! Is something going on? This isn't like you!"

Of course, it's like me. I screw up everything according to my mother. I sighed heavily and rubbed my temples in irritation. "I don't know what you want me to say, Mr. Martin -"

"I want you to say you'll try harder. You have seven missing assignments. You show up late to my class or don't show up at all. You're way past the verge of failing."

"Okay, so why try?!" I asked, getting irritated.

"Because I can help you but you gotta start to care. You're heading down a dangerous road."

The road of what? Failure? Pretty sure we're already heading down that road."Are we done?"

He looked at me with eyes that showed I was unrecognizable. He didn't expect this and now I feel like a terrible person. I'm just mad at the entire world and I'm taking it out on him.

Mr. Martin sighed but motioned that I could step out of his class. I do so. I make sure to grab everything before heading out of the room.

His voice stops me. "If you show up late to my class again, Amara; I will fail you and you will have to repeat the 12th grade."

I didn't care. I just headed straight out of the class.

Why does it matter so much that I'm not trying? I'm only doing what my mother taught me. It's better to not try at all than to fail once in life.

My mind then starts to rest on how I acted toward Mr. Martin and how much of a terrible person I felt for it. I don't know why I acted like that. I just did it.

Jean, my newfound friend and also the girl that's known as more popular came up to me. "Amara! You look..." She examines my outfit and a disdainful look comes up which she quickly hides with a smile. "Yourself."

I hold myself back from rolling my eyes. "When's Wyatt's party?"

"Tonight. Be there before ten though."

"Bet."

"Derek is going to be there. And he's got his eyes on you."

I never really cared for relationships so even the thought of this didn't phase me at all. Also, Derek wasn't the best guy and I knew that. He used women around him and didn't care for them. I wasn't stupid. "Derek is going to be disappointed then."

Jean gave me a look like she couldn't believe what I had just said. "You don't want Derek? Thee Derek?"

I scoff at her. "Oh, he's thee, Derek, now? He'll be fine without me."

Later on that night, I had little to convince my mom of me going to the party. She didn't care. Just gulped down her last beer in silence.

It was getting more of a routine. Her just not being there for me. I was starting to get used to it.

The house was on the eastside of Detroit. Not exactly the safest time at night to be walking on your own but I did it anyway. I walked up to the house and knocked on the door.

To my surprise, Derek had opened the door. "Glad you could make it."

I couldn't help but make a little eye roll before sliding past him. Jean came up to hug me. "Amara!" She pulls away. "Glad you could make it."

"Me too," Wyatt says. I don't know why but the way Wyatt said that it seemed like he had another meaning behind it. He couldn't though. This was Jean's boyfriend.

Wyatt walked over to me and handed me a couple of pills. "Here take these."

I raised a brow at this. "What are they?"

"Xanax. They'll make you mellow out."

Something in my head screamed not to do it but another part of me wanted to fit in. Everyone else was doing it. I felt like I had to do it.

I took the xanax and threw them in my mouth and chugged them down with the can of beer Wyatt handed me. "Gross."

Wyatt chuckled. "You'll be fine. Trust me."

Jean takes my hand and brings me to the circle. We all sat down. "Okay, so we're all gonna play truth or dare."

Something about this just made me uncomfortable. I knew why we teenagers played truth or dare and I didn't want to be a part of it. I also didn't want to seem like a party crasher so I just decided to go along with it. "Okay, who's first?"

"You," Jean states simply. "Truth or dare Amara?"

"Dare," I said confidently.

Jean has this devious look on her face. "Alright, I dare you to kiss Derek."

Are you kidding me? I just told her I had no interest in Derek. So, why was she pushing it? I saw the look on Derek's face. He was waiting for this. And it made me sick. My anxiety kicked in. "No. Do another one."

"Oh come on, Amara." Derek wraps his arm around my shoulders. "Don't be such a downer."

He starts leaning into me and I push him off. "I need some air."

Some of the kids, even Jean, were 'booing' me because I didn't do it. I don't care. I'm not like this. This isn't me. I had to keep telling myself that over and over again.

I was in a separate room now just trying to calm my breathing. Wyatt came into the room. "Hey, sorry about that. That was lame for them to do."

Finally, someone that understood my situation. "Thank you. It's just weird for me to do that. Derek isn't my type."

"I get it," Wyatt says to me. He walks over and sits on the bed. "If you need anything I'm always here."

"Thank you, Wyatt. I appreciate it."

"Always." He places his hand on my thigh.

He was Jean's boyfriend so why was he touching me like this? "What are you doing?"

"You know I'm nothing like Derek right?" Wyatt questioned ignoring my own.

"I mean...I guess." I started to feel calmer. My nerves weren't there anymore. I started to feel even sleepy and I had gathered it was the side effect of the pill.

"You and I both know we look good together. Just forget about Jean."

Wyatt started to lean in closer to me. I don't know what I was thinking. I leaned in and I kissed him. I know I shouldn't have. I don't know why I did it. It was just me and him in the room and I felt like I had to since he was being so nice to me.

Jean came into the room. "What's going on?"

Before I could speak, Wyatt pulled away and spoke. "I don't know babe. She just started to come onto me."

"What?!" Jean and I shouted in unison. He had to be joking. No way he just tried to blame this all on me.

"Yeah, what were you saying, Amara?" Wyatt asked rhetorically. "How we would look good together and we should just forget about Jean?"

"Oh really?" Jean questioned angrily.

"No, that's not what happened!" I countered. "He's the one who did it! Not me. J, you gotta believe me. We're friends."

Jean scoffs at my claim. "Friends? I barely know you. I took you in because you were so gloomy, sad, and so freaking miserable that you were making everybody else miserable. I tried to do the right thing and look where that got me. My back stabbed!"

I tried to hold back the tears. I made everyone depressed? I was that miserable I made everyone else feel that way too?

I walked out of the party and went back to my house.

Chapter Two
MY OWN REFLECTION

It was a long walk. I had to think about so many things. My friends weren't my friends. I already felt this pain inside of me but it only got worse when everything happened.

Why was my life such a mess?

Walking into my house, the first thing I see is my mom passed out on the couch. Of course, she was. What else was new?

I go to the bathroom to wash off all my makeup and to just clear my head a little.

I looked in the mirror. Then I looked back at my mother. My mother was drugged out on the couch, mascara running down her rosy red cheeks. I looked back in the mirror, my mascara running down my rosy red cheeks.

I preached so loudly I would never become like the woman that birthed me. I was mistaken. I am that woman. I am that monster that created me.

All I could do was cry. I messed everything up. I did this and I didn't know how to come up from it.

The next day I couldn't get out of bed. Depression and anxiety took over my body. My mom seemed to be in the same predicament because she didn't even go in for work today.

I decided it was time for me to get up. So, I did. I got up and got ready for school.

I went into the kitchen to get myself an apple and there was my mother who looked disappointed and all.

"Going to add school dropout to the list of things you've done?"

Great. She was down from her high and I had to deal with it. "Thanks, mom."

"You didn't do your hair, your clothes are dirty, are you even taking care of yourself? It's pathetic really."

"Again, thanks, mom." This was all routine for me. I was used to being my mother's biggest failure.

Going to school was horrible. Whispers were spoken in the halls about me and Wyatt. How I was dirty for what I had done in his story.

He was right. I shouldn't have even taken the pill he gave me. If I didn't then none of this would ever happen.

I'm such a terrible person.

I tried to walk into Mr. Martin's class but the door was locked. That was weird. His door was never locked. I knocked on the door and then waited a couple of seconds.

Mr. Martin opened the door but stopped me from walking in. "I warned you, Amara."

I was confused. Then I thought about our conversation but I didn't believe him to be serious. "Wait okay, I know I messed up but -"

"There are no buts, Amara. I gave you that warning. I can't keep saving someone that doesn't want to be saved." He tells me. He doesn't look me in the eye while doing so. "You failed this class and you have to repeat the 12th grade. Go to the office and get a pass."

Then he just closes his door.

My heart dropped. My stomach was in my throat. I couldn't breathe. This couldn't be happening.

'Oh, now you want to care, Amara? When it's all set in stone?' My thoughts churned.

I see Jean laughing with her friends as she points to me. This was it. This was the last straw.

I threw my bookbag to the ground and walked over to her. "Oh hey, Amara," Jean says all sweetly. "I was just-"

I didn't give her any time. I punched her in her jaw and she fell to the ground. I then bent down and started to beat her face repeatedly over and over again.

What else did I have to lose?

"You're expelled."

After the fight, I was pulled off by Mr. Martin and some other teachers. Now I was in the principal's office with Ms. Preston. I knew her personally because she was my mom's ex-best friend. They don't talk anymore for obvious reasons.

I guess everything could get worse.

"You know this school has zero tolerance for fighting." Ms. Preston said.

Great. Now I have no school.

I put on a tough act and just shrugged my shoulders. "Whatever."

Ms. Preston tilts her head. I think she could see through my act. I did care. Deep down I did. I just don't know how to show it.

Sometimes I get this anger inside me. It's this rage that I can't stop. Or maybe I can. I'm just making up excuses.

I'm such a terrible person.

"Listen..." Ms. Preston starts to say. "You're eighteen so you're grown up enough for this talk." She crosses her hands together and leans over the desk. "This world out here doesn't care about you."

"Good thing I don't care about the world huh?" I couldn't help the smart remark roll off my tongue.

Ms. Preston ignores it. "You can't keep giving up just because things get hard. If anything you need to push through those hardships and learn from it. Even if it takes a little bit of failing."

I don't say anything. I just look at her. Maybe she was right. This was all my fault and I had to fix it. "How? How do I fix something that is already broken?"

She sighs. "This is your last chance." She takes out a paper from her desk and hands it to me. "This place is called Detroit Job Corps. I think it will be a good fresh start for you. I suggest you get your act together or end up like your mother."

It clicked. The reminder of my mother sunk into my head. The image of her being nothing, sleeping on the couch with no purpose in my life.

It scared me.

I had to get it together. I couldn't be like her. I can't be like her.

I grabbed the pamphlet and looked at it. Detroit Job Corps center.

This was my shot. My last chance.

Chapter Three
A PAIN WORSE THAN DEATH

When I told my mother I was expelled from school, I was expecting an "I knew it." The occasional "I knew you'd always be a failure." Even an "you failed school and you're going to fail at life." She didn't though. She just looked at me like I was stone. A piece of nothing. Then she went on to continue to do the dishes.

Maybe she was so disappointed in me that she couldn't even speak to me. Maybe her drugs made her go mute. Maybe she was really just sick of me.

That's when I told her that I was going to the Detroit Job Corps. That shook her to her core. "Away from home? Away from me? No you're not!"

I didn't understand it. It's not like she ever cared about my well being. Why all of the sudden did she care now? Not to mention I was eighteen which meant she legally couldn't stop me.

"Oh, now you want to be a mother? A bit too late for that don't you think?" I sneered.

My mother was fuming. It's like she couldn't believe I could talk back. Usually I'd just agree with her like a good child. Not anymore. I was done with it. I was done with her.

She held her breath. Probably from her being so angry. Then she let that breath out and looked at me. "I've been going through a really rough time, Amara."

I actually could not believe her. She was going through a rough time? Was the rough time popping pills so she could barely wake up?

I laughed. I was so tired of everything and the long day I had. Most people would be crying and usually I would be too but I think that I was just so tired that I couldn't take it anymore. I was just laughing.

Mom looked at me like I was crazy. She was just watching her daughter laugh at her. Like it was the funniest thing in the world. "What's so funny?"

She was mad and it honestly brought some type of joy out of me. I didn't even realize that my laughter started to turn into tears. I was exhausted.

"You're right mom. You have been going through a rough time. For eighteen years! Eighteen years you've been going through such a rough time. I mean don't you think it gets a little old to feel sorry for yourself? All I ever have been to you is a failure. That's all I'll ever be so why do you want me here mom? What do you really want?"

That's when it hit me. She didn't care about me being far away from home. She wouldn't be worried sick. This was about control. She wouldn't have a say in my life choices. She would have nothing left.

"Oh my god." I held my hand to my throat, clutching it at the realization. I gave her the deadliest stare known to man. "This isn't about you loving me. This is about control. You just want to control me for the rest of your life. Well that's not happening. You don't get to control what I will be because I will be something. Not the failure that you have in your mind and there's nothing you can do to stop it."

I think that's what snapped my mother into her Bipolar episode. She started to smash things around the house. The vase, the TV, the table, everything. She continued to smash things and I just stood there and took it.

She even started to throw the pillows from the couch at me. Again, I stood there and took it. "You ungrateful little brat!" She threw the table across the room. "All I've ever done was be the best mom I can be and this is how you repay me?"

Mom started to punch the walls as she threw her fit. I just stood there and watched. "I hate this! I hate you!" She seemed too out of breath to continue.

"Are you done?" I asked her.

"Am I done? Am I done? I'm just getting started!" She threw one last thing, which was the lamp across the room, right at the direction of my head but it missed.

Tears ran down my face as I watched my mom fall apart. "Tears Amara? Don't act like you care." She starts clapping her hands sarcastically as if I needed a standing ovation from my very real tears that she believed to be fake. "What you want a B.E.T award or something?"

I was done. I walked out of that house. I heard from behind me "don't you think about ever coming back." My mom always said that when we had a fight so I didn't think much of it.

I've never been more exhausted before in my entire life. I dealt with the horrible woman since birth because my father was barely around. So, that meant I had to deal with her. I didn't want this life anymore. I couldn't do it anymore.

I decided to get a cup of coffee at the local coffee shop just to clear my head a little. I went up to the counter and paid for my Ice Cappuccino. That's when I saw Wyatt at a table sitting with his friends. He was laughing like there wasn't a care in the world. I turned around quickly hoping he didn't see me. He did.

"Hey, Amara!" I cursed under my breath and turned around to see a very angry Wyatt walking up to me. "Want to explain to me why you attacked my girlfriend?"

"Oh now she's your girlfriend?" I questioned. "You know it would be nice if I could get a schedule of the days you and Jean are together. That would be great so I won't get confused." I said sarcastically.

"Do I have to remind you that you kissed me back?"

"You gave me xanax!"

"Which you willingly took!"

He had a point. It was my choice to take the drug. I wasn't forced to. I forced myself. That I couldn't blame him for. "Fine, whatever."

I grabbed my drink and tried to walk away but Wyatt grabbed my arm roughly and forced me into place. "We're not done here."

I was actually pretty terrified. Wyatt was 5'8 and on the football team. He could easily overpower me. The grip on my arm tightened and I hissed in pain. "Wyatt, you're hurting me."

"Everything okay?" We turn to the voice. It was a boy. Around the same age as me. He was even taller than Wyatt.

At least 6 feet. He looked like he worked out more than Wyatt. I could tell Wyatt was scared of him but he hid it with an angry expression.

"This doesn't concern you." Wyatt told him.

Before the boy could even speak, Derek had walked over to Wyatt. "Wyatt come on. Let's go. That's Zane Reese."

"So?"

"I'll tell you on the way."

Derek and Wyatt walk away. I was left confused. Why was Derek so scared of this guy? How did he know this guy? I never even saw him going to our school.

I look at the boy. What should I say? Thank you? "I didn't need your help."

The boy looked at me unconvinced and his eyes went to the bruise now forming on my arm. "Right." He holds out his hand for me to shake. "I'm Zane."

I grabbed my Iced Capp and pushed past him. "That's great that you have a name."

Instead of getting mad, he laughed. I wasn't expecting that. I was expecting him to curse me out but instead he laughed. "Cute."

We walked out of the Tim Hortons. When I saw he was still following me I rolled my eyes. "Is there something I can help you with? Or is stalking young girls in a coffee shop on your list of things to do for the day?"

He seemed amused at my sarcasm which annoyed me to no end. "I'm just trying to make sure you're okay."

"I'm okay. You can go now."

The boy, Zane, tilted his head at me. "You know I'm not like those other guys right."

I couldn't help but scoff. "Yeah, I heard that one before. People like you are the reason why I'm mad at the world."

"Mad at the world huh? Let me guess...bad day?"

"More like a bad decade."

Zane laughed. "Yeah, well I can relate but it doesn't help to mope about it for the rest of your life. What's the point of living if all you have to say for yourself is negative stuff?"

He was right. Life was tough enough as it is. Being negative about everything wouldn't help. Especially my own personal negativity. "You're right."

"I tend to be right all the time."

I rolled my eyes. "And I'm leaving." I turned to walk away but he had called me back.

"I can't get a name?"

I turn around, still walking. "If we see each other again, I'll tell you."

Walking back home, I felt better. I was going to have a good long talk with my mom and everything might not exactly be okay but it would be better.

When I got to my house my heart dropped. All my stuff was set on the front porch. I ran to the porch and saw there was a note.

'I told you not to come back. '

My mother and I always got into arguments. She always said that she'd kick me out. I just never believed that she would ever do it.

Great. I'm homeless now and I wouldn't be able to get into Job Corps for at least 3 months. All I could do was sit on that porch and cry.

Chapter Four
BELIEVE IN YOURSELF

2 MONTHS LATER

I actually couldn't believe that I finally got into the Detroit Job Corps. I got the call and they said to come on Tuesday at 8 for the first day.

I had been homeless for 2 months and it seemed like things were finally going my way. It was a victory that I had to celebrate. I had to quit my job because I couldn't work and be on campus at the same time. It was just a team member at the local coffee shop.

Taking everything I owned would be impossible. Some of the things I had got lost while me being homeless so I had very few things to begin with.

Deciding what was important and what I didn't need, I gave the rest away to a homeless shelter and took what I could carry before making my way to Detroit Job Corp.

I wasn't expecting the security gates or being questioned. They had to search me before I could even think about entering the program and search my stuff. They did not play about weapons or drugs. I figured one too many students brought it on campus.

Once the search was finished I had to sit down and wait with four other students. My nerves started to act up. When I saw how everyone was dressed I felt like I was underdressed. Girls had their makeup done, their outfits matching and smiling like they actually belonged there.

Maybe I didn't belong here. Maybe I didn't have a purpose being here.

The doors opened and a man walked in. Maybe this was finally where I could get some information. "Sorry for the wait." He tells us. "I'm Mr. Singal but you can call me Mr. S. My name is not hard to pronounce though." He kinda laughs at what he says before continuing. "I'm going to be your CPP teacher. You guys won't be seeing me until tomorrow. Today you have to go to Wellness center which you'll be in all day."

The girl next to me raises her hand. "What's Wellness and why are we going to be there all day?"

"Good question." He says before responding. "It's basically the nurses station at school and they need to do some tests on you. See if there's anything they should be concerned about."

We all went to wellness and it was a long day. They took our blood and ran all types of tests on us. It would be fine if it was one, maybe two hours but we have to stay there for the whole day. From 8 to 3:30.

When it came 11 o'clock, it was time for lunch. I wasn't looking forward to it. Being around a lot of people. Having people see me sit by myself. I didn't think about any of this before moving to Job Corp.

Two students were supposed to be giving us a tour. One girl walked in. "Hey, I'm Larisa. And this is.." She turns to look behind her but the person she was talking about wasn't there. "Oh my god. Where did he go?"

"I'm here." There he was. The boy I met at the Tim Hortons.

"You have got to be kidding me..." I mumbled.

Zane looked at me and a smile came on his face. "Oh hey, it's the coffee girl."

There's no way that this was real. I had to be hallucinating due to exhaustion. No way Zane, the boy I met two months ago, went here to Detroit Job Corps.

"Coffee girl?" The girl, Larisa, questioned.

"It's Amara." I say, now forced to tell him my name.

He seemed content with my answer. He knew not to push it though. He motioned his hand out. "I'll take you guys to lunch."

We walk down the halls. Zane kept talking throughout the walk. I pegged him to be a people person. He was just so joyful and full of life that it was sort of frightening. I never met someone that was so positive before in my entire life. Maybe because all I've been surrounded by was negative.

I decided not to eat lunch that day. I was too nervous and my stomach wouldn't calm down. I took that as an opportunity to examine the people around me.

There were a bunch of loud personalities. People that tried to prove that they were tough. People that were fake. It was exactly like high school. It made me lose some hope. If I couldn't even finish high school, how was I supposed to finish this?

Then I started to feel embarrassed that I was sitting by myself which only made my anxiety heighten. This was going to be harder than I thought.

That's when Zane sat next to me with a plate of food in his hands. "Why aren't you eating?"

"Not hungry." I said blandly to him.

He nods understandingly. "Too anxious to eat?"

I looked at him, surprised he guessed it. I then looked back to my phone. "Yeah."

"So, how did you end up here?"

I figured he wasn't going to leave me alone so I might as well talk to him. I sighed before responding. "I got expelled from my old school. For fighting this one girl."

Zane didn't seem to expect that. "Really?"

"You think I'm lying?"

"No. It's just you're so quiet. Wouldn't expect that from you." He leaned back in his seat. "Then again, quiet girls get fed up."

"Yeah, let's just say I was having a really bad day." It came to my mind what Derek had said the day we met and if he got to question me, I got to question him. "Why was Derek so scared of you? And how did he know you?"

Zane was uncomfortable by my question. I could tell which flabbergasted me. I never thought he could get uncomfortable but he was. He had to answer my question though since he had been questioning me. "Before Job Corp, I was a really bad guy doing really bad things."

I raised an eyebrow at him. "Is that the polite way of saying you were in a gang?"

He chuckles but it's an awkward chuckle. I can tell he was embarrassed by his past. It was refreshing he was telling me. He felt like the first real person that I could talk to. "Yeah...that."

"That's why he was so scared of you." I look him up and down. "You don't look so scary."

Zane laughs. "Glad to know you're not scared of me." He tells me. "Still think the world is out to get you?"

How did he remember that about me? I barely could remember his name. Maybe that really shows how conceited I am.

"Well you're still talking to me so yes, the world is out to get me."

My rudeness didn't drive him away. He was amused by it actually. "But you're still talking to me so is it that bad?"

Zane talking to me was better than sitting alone by myself. He wasn't bad to talk to either. My nerves were actually disappearing because of the conversation. I didn't want to boost his ego so I continued to stare down at my phone.

He didn't seem to mind the silence. He slid his tray of food to me and handed me the fork and spoon for the food. "I'll be back." He said before getting up and what I assume to go get another tray of food.

I took a bite, smiling to myself. I wasn't anxious to eat my food anymore. It was like I felt better.

Chapter Five
IT GETS TOUGHER FROM HERE

Later on in the day, we finally finished with Wellness and were on our way to the dorms. Before I could take my clothes inside my dorm we had to dry them and do inventory. It was a safety precaution I guess.

When I was done I got to go inside my room. There were three girls, including the girl I came here with, in their beds. "Hey, it's one of the new girls."

I hated the attention being on me but I know sulking about it would get me nowhere. I just put on my best fake smile. "Hey guys."

One of the girls got up from her bed and walked over to me. "I'm Ashanti." She points over to the other girl who wouldn't dare look my way. "That's Hannah."

The new girl waved at me. "I'm Zaria."

"I'm Amara." I introduced myself.

"We were just about to go to dinner if you want to go down with us." Ashanti said to me.

I smiled at the offer. "That would be great. Let me just put my clothes up and I'll meet you there."

"Alright bet."

Ashanti and Zaria walked out of the room. Hannah still sat on her bed without saying a single word to me. I felt like I was obligated to talk to her since we were roommates.

I started to hang my clothes up and speak. "So, how long have you been at Job Corp?"

Hannah huffed at me and got up from her bed. She started to walk closer to me as if to try and intimidate me. I wasn't easily intimidated though. "Look, we're not going to be friends so stop trying."

I was confused. I just got here. How did I already make an enemy? "I'm not understanding."

Well, if I didn't understand she was going to make me understand. "You were talking with Zane. I saw you. He's my man so get a grip and leave him alone."

Oh. My. God.

Why is the center problem always a boy when it comes to me? Am I really that awful?

"Look, I didn't know -" I tried to explain but she wasn't having it.

"Well now you do." She says to me, "Stay away from him and stay away from me.."

Hannah walks out the room. I couldn't help but feel bad. I hadn't even done anything and I already made an enemy. Once again, Job Corp was going to be harder than I thought.

Instead of sadness it turned into rage. How dare she treat me like this? Over some boy? The only person that had been genuinely nice to me my entire stay here? Now I couldn't even talk to him anymore?

I wanted to do what my mom always did. Freak out. Throw everything across the room. Slam the doors. Do something, anything but instead I kept it all bottled in. I couldn't be like her. I can't be like her.

I decided to just go to dinner by myself. I didn't want any problems with Hannah or even her friends. So, I grabbed my tray of food and was about to head to a table. That was until Hannah walked over to me. She smeared the nachos all over my clothes. I gasped. Not even by the heat of the food but out of surprise.

She was really going to do this?

Everyone turned towards us. I think Hannah was expecting laughter. I was too. Like some cheesy 90s romcom but nobody laughed. Not a single person did. Everyone was just in silence.

This was my first day and I already was over it. This wasn't for me. I think it was my impulsiveness talking but I'd rather be homeless than to stay here another minute.

Screwing things up was my specialty wasn't it?

I went to punch her in the face but I felt a hand stop me. It was Zane. "Don't do it." He told me. "Let's get you cleaned up." Zane led me away from the scene.

We walked over to the dorms. Zane waited for me in the common area. I changed out of my clothes and held back my tears. How was I supposed to go through the job corp with Hannah as my roommate?

This just wasn't going to work.

I walked into the common area and sat next to Zane. He sighed. He almost seemed embarrassed at what had happened. "I'm sorry about Hannah. She's still hung up over the breakup."

That enraged me. I gave him a look. "You mean I got nachos thrown on me by a girl who's not even your girlfriend?"

"Pretty much."

I can't stand this place.

"Look." He begins to speak. "You almost hit her. And you know that would've meant you being out of the program."

I shrugged. "I'll suck at this program anyway. What's the point?"

"Well, how do you know if you won't try? I used to be the same way. I didn't want to be here. I was sick of everyone. I thought I couldn't do it but look at me. I completed my trade. Now I just need my high school diploma."

"Lucky you." I say sarcastically. "But you weren't the one that had nachos thrown on in front of the whole school so I think I get to sulk about this one."

"You're right. You do get to sulk." He said. "But soon you're going to have to pick yourself back up. You can't let what others do interrupt your opportunities."

I looked up at him and just gave him a look. "You sound like a teacher."

"Oh shut up."

I laughed with him. Talking to Zane was refreshing. I never heard so much positivity before in my life. He was right. I could do this.

I had to do this.

Chapter Six
SOMETHING OUT OF NOTHING

For three weeks we would have to be with our CPP teacher Mr. S. It actually wasn't bad at all. Mr. S was actually a pretty relaxed and laid back teacher but he didn't allow disrespect or for people to walk all over him. I admire that about him.

There were four other students in the class. My roommate Zaria. She was usually angry all the time. Anything could ruin her day. If her day was ruined, she would make sure your day was ruined too. For some reason, I didn't really mind her anger. I was okay with being friends with her.

There was Tabitha. She talked a lot and was really energetic. She always seemed to have a smile on her face and a compliment for everyone ready at hand. I found her happiness to be an illusion. Something just wasn't right about her. Then again, maybe I'm just not used to positivity.

Enzo was alright. He was pretty laid back and didn't like drama. His biggest thing that he would constantly remind us is respect. He didn't appreciate anyone disrespecting him or the people around him.

Finally there was Sebastian. He didn't seem like the brightest person. Always trying to prove that he was the toughest guy at Detroit Job Corp which I couldn't help but roll my eyes at the seventeen year old. I wasn't really sure why people wanted to be popular at the school full of screw ups but hey, that's just me I guess.

All together, the class didn't seem that bad. We all pretty much respected Mr. S and listened to him. There really weren't any problems with him. I was actually doing well in the class. I finished with MyPace, a piece of the CPP curriculum, so I didn't really have anything to do.

Mr. S informed us that we would TABE test on Thursday and Friday. Basically it was a math and reading test and you needed to score a certain amount in order to not have a reading or math class. I'm not exactly smart. Especially at math so I knew I wouldn't be able to test out.

Sometimes I hated how stupid I was. My intelligence was down the drain. I tried to think back on why I always perceived myself as dumb. Then I remembered. My oh so wonderful mother.

I still haven't spoken to my mother. It was clear that our relationship was destroyed. There was no way it would be able to come up from below. Not after everything she's done to me. Not after her kicking me out.

Zaria and I sat at lunch together. She was going on and on about Sebastian and how they were made for each other. I just decided that agreeing with her and moving on would be for the best because telling her it was a bad idea wouldn't stop her.

As we ate, Zaria gave me a smirk as if she had something waving over in her mind. "So, you and Zane?"

I wasn't that dumb. I knew what she was implying and I was not having it. Boys brought nothing more than pain and sorrow and that's not something I wanted. No matter how much of a good guy I thought Zane was.

Zane and I were pretty good friends. He was always there for me to help me change my perspective on the world. I'd like to believe that I did the same for him.

"No, there is no me and Zane. I don't want to think about boys. Just want to get my high school diploma, get my trade, and be done with this program for good."

"I feel that. My attention is strictly on my education." She lied.

"Yeah, sure it is." I let her have it not even wanting to do the whole back and forth thing with her.

Zaria caught on and decided to change the subject. "What do you think you'll do on your TABE tests?"

I sighed at the thought of it. "Probably fail. I don't know. It just seems hard."

That's when Zaria gave me this look. Like a disappointed mother. "Are you always this negative?"

The mention of that made me think back on Jean's words. How I was so miserable I made everyone else miserable. I looked down to my food, ashamed of my traits. "Trying to break that."

Zaria usually was rude and I knew she didn't mean anything by it so I didn't take it into consideration that she was purposefully being mean.

We continued to eat our food. I could see Hannah from across the room with her friends. She was staring at me. Then began to whisper to the girls and laughed.

The faculty didn't know about Hannah putting nachos all over me and I wasn't going to tell them and be known as a snitch at the school. Life was already hard enough as it was so I wasn't going to make it harder.

I tried to take Zane's advice and just take the high road but it was hard when all your life you felt like you had to defend yourself.

We were back in Mr. S's class. I didn't really know why I called him Mr. S when I knew how to pronounce his last name. Maybe it was because everyone else called him that.

Everyone worked on their MyPace while I just worked on my resume. I already had one but I wanted a fresh resume in the system. That's when my phone rang. It was an unknown number.

I raised my hand. "May I answer this phone call?"

Mr. S motioned for me to go outside the classroom. "Of course, you can."

I nodded and stood up. Then walked out the classroom. I was still confused. Who could be calling me? I didn't know many people and why did I not know this number? I answered the phone with caution. "Hello?"

"Is this Amara?" It was a deep, rough voice. The man sounded like he smoked cigarettes every day. The voice also sounded familiar but I couldn't put my finger on it.

"Yes. Who is this?"

"It's your father."

My heart sank. It went to the bottom of my stomach. I hadn't spoken to my father in six months. Now all of the sudden he decided to give me a call? He must need something. "I don't have any money for you. I'm broke."

"That's not why I called." He said, almost offended that I would even say that. "We need to have a talk. Do you have a minute?"

"Not really. I'm in class." I say, already annoyed by talking to him.

"Oh, you're in class. The last time I spoke to your mother she said you were expelled."

"Long story. What do you want?"

I heard a deep breath being taken from the phone. I raised a brow. I never heard my dad being so serious before. Whatever he had to tell me must've been important.

"Your mother is dead."

My blood ran cold. This can't be right. My mother couldn't be dead. She can't be dead. "What?" There had to be some mistake. Then I realized that it was stupid of me to not think she had it coming. She was a mentally ill drug addict. She probably just overdosed. "How?"

"She killed herself."

There was no way that was right. My selfish waste excuse of a mother? Suicide? No, they had to have gotten it wrong. "No. That's not right. How would you even come to that conclusion."

"There's a suicide note. She took a whole bottle of pills. They tried doing everything they could but there was nothing they could do."

I held back the tears that threatened to come down my cheeks. No, I wouldn't cry for this woman. She didn't deserve my tears. "Okay. Thank you for telling me."

"Now, hold on a second." My dad said. "The funeral is this Friday. At two o'clock. Going to be at Sandy Beach."

I scoffed at the idea. "A funeral at a beach? What is this a beach party?"

"She'll be buried at the local cemetery. I'd also like to spend some time with you before the funeral."

"Are you serious? It's a bit late to earn father of the year don't you think? Do you even know the life I've had without you? I've only seen you five times out of my entire life. Five. You think the death of my mom makes up for everything? I was homeless for two months. Why may you ask? Because my mom kicked me out and guess where you were? Nowhere! Anywhere but being in my life. So, do what you do best; stay away from me."

I hung up the phone and took a breath. Life just keeps getting harder and harder.

My phone buzzed. I looked to see I received a text message from him.

"Here's her suicide note if you want to read it."

I refused to look at it. I wasn't going to give my mother the satisfaction that I, her daughter, read her pathetic suicide letter. I was going to go back into class, do my work, and focus on my life.

Chapter Seven
CARVE YOUR HEART OUT

When the school day was over, I just went back to my dorms and isolated myself. Hearing the news of my mother didn't make me want to come out. I figured I would just study for my TABE test. I did not want a math and reading class. It would just get in the way of me being in high school diploma.

I wanted to finish this program as fast as I could and the two classes would just get in the way. I didn't want the long way. I wanted to take the short cut. This was that very short cut.

Hannah was arguing with Zane over FaceTime. This was an everyday experience for me. It was starting to get annoying. All she did was complain about why they weren't together. She couldn't realize that she was a self serving psychopath and nobody wanted to be with her.

Listening to their conversation just made me want to pull my hair out but she was my roommate. I had no choice but to listen to the outrageous conversation. May I add, the most stupid conversation I heard in a while.

When Zane said Hannah was obsessed with him, he wasn't kidding. The girl could not take no for an answer and I was starting to see the hundred reasons why he broke up with the girl. "Why can't you just go to the color party with me?" She asked.

"Because we're not together anymore, Hannah. How many times do I have to tell you?"

"I saw you talking to Larisa today. Why was that?"

"Let's see. By my calculations I don't need to inform you why I talk to other girls because you're not my girlfriend."

I couldn't help but snicker. My sarcasm was starting to rub off on him. It was funny. Hannah though, was not amused. Even more irritated than ever. "Ugh!"

Hannah hung up the phone and threw it on her bed. Zaria walked into the room. She looked at me and sighed. "You're still studying?! Mr. S said that it's pointless. Nobody TABES' out on the first try."

"Well, I'm going to try."

Zaria held her hands up in defense. "Hey, I'm just saying there's no use to straining your brain over it."

That's when Hannah turned to us and smirked. "You know, I TABED out on the first try in reading."

"Yeah right." I said to her, not believing her.

She looked livid. "I did! It was easy. Let's hope you can do the same." She says smartly before walking out the room.

I was mad. There was no way I was going to let Hannah have one up on me. I had to TABE out. No matter what. Zaria could see how mad it made me and she shook her head. "This isn't going to end good."

It was like Hannah and I were in some type of competition. It didn't matter what it was, we were always up against each other and I was going to win.

"You're not going to the color party?" Zaria asked as she started to change out of her clothes.

I shrugged. "You know I don't do social events."

"Okay. Whatever you say."

I was good on parties after the last party I went to. I ended up taking drugs and then kissing my ex friend's boyfriend. Plus, I wasn't so social anyway.

I couldn't help but think about the note my father had sent me. I know I said I wouldn't look at it but I honestly didn't think I couldn't. I had to see what the woman wrote before deciding to kill herself.

This was going to be a bad idea. I would regret it. I knew I would. Something in me told me I had to do it. Like I deserved to read my mother's final thoughts before her passing.

I got out my phone and went to the text message.

Dear Amara,

I don't even know how to start this letter. I know I wasn't always a good mom to you or even a good person. I know you hate me and I wish I could change that. I wish I could change the way you think of me. You think I believe you're a failure? A disappointment even? Truth is you are the very failure I believe you are. Want to know why? Because you're Amara Williams. You are destined for disappointment. I can't even tell you why I did it. I was just so miserable that I made everyone else miserable. Maybe I deserve this. Eternal despair. You feel that rage in you Amara? That darkness? The very thing inside you that makes you hate the world? You can't bury it. You have to live in it. You will never be anything great. That's not necessarily your fault. That's just something you have to live with. I'm not asking for much. Just for your forgiveness for being a horrible mom to you.

Mom.

I cried. How dare she do this? How dare she take the easy way out? Life gets hard but I didn't quit. I didn't give up. Not like she did. And what was this? This poor excuse of a letter. Telling me I'm destined for disappointment?

It was different hearing it from a letter. Yes, I heard it from her mouth all my life but her last thoughts were this? She felt like she had to include this in the letter. What was she trying to do? To hurt me? Well, mission accomplished because she did it.

There was one thing she was right about. I did have this rage inside me. I was mad at everything. At the whole world. All this did was make the fire grow greater.

One thing in my mind clicked for me. She said she was so miserable that she made other people miserable. I couldn't help but think to myself about that. There's no way we could relate to the subject. She was an abusive woman while I was a teen just mad at the world. We weren't the same.

We can't be the same.

My phone started to ring. It was Zane. I didn't want to talk to him right now. I didn't want him to see me like this. I just declined the call, curled up into the ball, and slowly started to fall asleep.

Right back into my old depression.

Chapter Eight
DOWN THIS ROAD

Two days had passed and I took the TABE test for both tests. I thought I did well on the tests. Especially the reading test. Mr. Stewart came into our class and explained our TABE test scores before we would be able to see them.

I was excited. I had to pass the tests. I opened the paper and looked at the scores.

A 514 in math and 562 in reading. I didn't pass the scores. I would have to take a reading and math test.

I think that I was so tired of failing that I couldn't hold it in anymore. I broke down crying. In class. I never felt more embarrassed before in my entire life but I did it. I was officially crying in class.

I made sure to do it quietly where hopefully nobody would notice me. Hopefully.

Turns out Mr. S noticed it. He got up from his desk and tapped me on the shoulder. "Let's go out in the hallway." We walked out in the hallway and he shut the door. He turns to look at me with eyes full of concern. "What's wrong?"

Usually, I didn't feel comfortable talking about my feelings but Mr. S made me feel safe and secure. I think it really didn't matter at this point either. I was just so stressed about everything that I blew up. "I wanted to prove I was smart. That I could TABE out but I couldn't and I didn't and now I'm just sitting here being the biggest disappointment that I'm destined to be."

Mr. S listened to my words carefully. I don't think he wanted to cut me off. He wanted to make sure I got everything off my chest before he spoke. "First of all, you're not a disappointment." He tells me. "Second of all, Amara, barely anyone scores enough on the tests on the first try. I warned you about that."

"I know I just - I just thought I was smarter than that."

"You are smart. And there's nothing wrong with you. Amara, you're one of the smartest kids I know. The test doesn't determine whether you're smart or not. Just show them what you need help with and what you're good at. Those scores don't define you as a person."

I sniffled. "Then what defines me as a person?"

"That's up to you to figure out."

I never really thought of it that way. I was so busy trying to rush my way into high school that I never really thought about the scores and how at the end of the day, they were just scores.

I thanked Mr. S and it was now finally the end of the day. I walked throughout the hallway and there I saw Zane. He spotted me. I turned around to try and get away from him but he followed me in an instant.

"Do you want to tell me why you've been avoiding me? Because I'd like to know-"

"Not in the mood, Zane."

"That's a coincidence because I'm not in the mood either. Guess we're both twinning."

"Wow, my sarcasm has really rubbed off on you. Go find someone else to copy because I'm not it."

I try to open the door to exit the academic building but he stops my hand and pulls me aside. "No. What's wrong? Did Hannah say something to you? Because I swear I-"

"My mom died." I blurted out, not knowing how else to say it. His anger calmed down and he finally was starting to feel understanding.

"I'm..." He tried to find the right words to say to me. "I'm sorry."

I shrugged, trying to seem like I didn't care. "You didn't kill her. She did it herself." He was taken back at what I said but I brushed it off. "Can you drive me somewhere after we get our weekend passes?"

The drive was long. We drove all the way to the cemetery around Sandy Beach. It was quiet. We didn't say a word to each other. It wasn't an awkward silence. It was more comfortable.

We pulled up to the cemetery. Zane parked the car. "I can stay here." He tells me.

I looked back at him. "I don't think I want to do this alone."

He nods understandingly and gets out of the car with me. We walked in the cemetery. I search and search for my mother's tombstone. There I see it. "In the loving memory of Edna Williams?" I read out loud. I couldn't believe I even had to read that. "So, what do I say?" I asked Zane.

Zane shrugged with concern. "Whatever you want."

I looked at the pot of dirt that covered my mother's coffin. I took in a deep breath and began to speak. "You told me that all you wanted from me was forgiveness. You want me to be this perfect daughter that thinks great things of you. So you can rest in peace."

I clenched my fists at the idea. I wanted to hold back but Zane said I could say whatever I wanted. I was going to do just that. "Well you're not getting that. You don't deserve peace. You don't deserve anything. Not the dollar in my pocket, not the gum off my shoe. Not my heart. Not my soul. Not everything that keeps me going."

"I tried so hard to be the best daughter I could be. I was your only child. How could you do this to me? And then you had the audacity to compare me to you? We're nothing alike! I have feelings. Emotions. I feel pain. Grief. You're a sociopath. You didn't want me to forgive you for me. You wanted it for yourself. God, you are the most self centered, egotistical person I've ever met. You ruin my life? And you're the one that gets to kill yourself?!"

"You deserve nothing but to rot! Like the disappointment you are. You're wrong, mom. I'm going to do great things. I'm going to be the best person I can be and I didn't need you to do it! Not you, not Dad, nobody. I can do this. I can be a better person without you. You are the very disappointment that rots within me."

I shook my head, not having anything more to say. I held back my tears for so long that I couldn't help but cry anymore. "Mom? Please. Please come back." I fell to the ground. My hands touched the dirt that buried her. It was cold. It felt like death upon me. "How could you do this to me?"

Zane watched me fall apart. It wasn't long until I felt his warm embrace around me. I cried in his arms as I questioned why this had to happen. Even after everything she put me through I couldn't help but feel grief.

That's when I realized that I'm not like her. I felt something.

Chapter Nine
KNOW YOUR WORTH

Conflict Resolution had to be the most stupid class that they could've given me. I did not need conflict resolution nor did I need any more classes in the way of getting my high school diploma. It was Monday and I was finally out of CPP. I had to admit that I was going to miss Mr. S and his instruction.

But Conflict Resolution? Why do I need this class and how would it help me in the future? I was annoyed to no end. I figured I would just be quiet in class, do the work, and that would be that. Maybe he wouldn't even notice me.

I heard a lot of people respected Mr. Moore. People rarely had anything negative to say about him. I wondered why they did that. He must not be a strict teacher.

Mr. Moore sat on the desk and looked around the room. "So, let's start." Everyone around the room started to put their phones and laptops away. Me and Zaria looked at each other and figured we'd do the same. "Goodmorning." He says to us.

"Goodmorning." We say back at him.

"Happy to see y'all beautiful faces today." He tells us. "I see we got some new faces. I'ma go around and one time. First name, tell me how you feel today."

Zaria was first. She giggles a little nervously. "Oh. Um. I'm Zaria and I feel alright."

It continues around the room until it eventually lands on me. I sighed, a little annoyed that I even had to participate in this. "Amara. I feel fine."

Mr. Moore has a smile on his face. Almost as if to mock me. "Just fine?"

"Yup."

"Okay then." He copies my sigh to mimic me. "Amara." The class chuckled a little and I couldn't help but roll my eyes. I was already over this class.

Mr. Moore walks up to the board and points to the words. "This week we're going to be working on self worth. In this world you gotta know your worth. Your worth is everything. It's what you believe your worth. And that's important."

He looks around the room and points to me. "Amara. What's your worth?"

Well, I guess being silent wasn't going to get me anywhere in this class. All eyes were on me. I hated the attention on me. Especially because I didn't know how to answer it.

Did I really not know my worth?

I never really thought of my worth as a whole. I definitely wouldn't be able to think of it with everybody looking at me waiting for my answer.

What did he want me to say? I didn't know the answer to my worth. Who would? We all didn't treat ourselves with respect. Why do you think we ended up at Detroit Job Corp?

"I don't know." I said.

Mr. Moore seemed to be a little disappointed in my answer. He just nods his head and points to me. "We'll work on that." And he continues on with his lesson.

When I was at lunch, Zaria laughed at Zane about my answer with Mr. Moore. "And then she just froze up and said." She sat with a blank expression. "I don't know." Then she laughed.

I rolled my eyes at her retelling the story to Zane. "Okay, okay. I get it."

Zane chuckled. "Your first mistake was being quiet. He loves to pick on the quiet kids."

"Gee. Thanks for the warning." I say sarcastically.

"Look, when he asks you again, what he wants you to say is you're smart, beautiful, important and needed."

I pause at those words. I never thought of myself as smart, beautiful, important or even needed. All my life I was told that I was dumb. I've been told I was ugly. I was the least important person around and needed? Nobody needed me.

Looking back at my food, I speak. "What if I don't believe those things about me?"

Zane and Zaria both look up at me. Zane looked like he was trying to find the right words and Zaria didn't seem to know what to say. Great. Now, I made the table awkward.

"I used to believe that too." Zane says. "I thought I was the dumbest person around. And I thought nobody needed me."

"What changed? How did you become the person that believed it?"

He shrugged. "I just found myself. When you find yourself, you'll start to believe in yourself."

I didn't know if I would ever find myself. That was asking a lot from me. Especially after everything that's happened to me.

Deep down I didn't know who I truly was. Would I be the mistakes that were engraved in my mother? Would I truly be the thing that terrified me?

I couldn't even be myself around other people. I felt like I had to be someone else because when people get to know the real me, nobody likes that version of me.

How do I find myself when I couldn't even be myself?

Zane rested his hand on my shoulder. "You'll figure it out."

Would I?

Zaria flipped her hair. "Me on the other hand? I'm very much smart, beautiful, important and needed."

Zane rolled his eyes. "Alright. We didn't need all that."

I heard people feed off your energy. You are what they are. The truth was I had gotten better after being around Zane and Zaria. I knew I wouldn't change completely. Change didn't come overnight but I think I am starting to get better with my positivity.

I just had to keep telling myself that I could do this. If I did that then nothing truly stood in my way. I would be invincible.

Chapter Ten
YOUR WORST ENEMY IS YOURSELF

Being back in Mr. Moore's class irritated my soul. I didn't want to be here. Stuck in a class that I shouldn't even have to take. I don't have anger issues. I know how to resolve conflict. Why did I need this stupid class?

It was Thursday. Apparently we play this game called *Hot Seat Thursday.'* Basically two people that don't really talk to each other sit across from each other and ask each other five questions on the stupid little piece of paper.

Mr. Moore looks around the room. I was begging for him not to pick me. Literally begging in my head. The begging in my head didn't work. "Amara and Yasmine."

Somebody kill me.

I sighed, getting out of my seat and heading towards the chair in the middle of the room. Yasmine, a girl I had no idea existed, copies my actions and sits in the other chair.

Mr. Moore hands us our sheet of paper. I skim over the questions I would have to ask her. Just dumb questions. "Pound it." He says, referring to us fist bumping.

We fist bump. I decided to go first. "Goodmorning, first and last name?"

"Yasmine White. Goodmorning, first and last name?"

"Amara Jones." Maybe if I just speed past the questions we can get it done quicker. "What's your favorite movie?" I questioned myself a little. These questions weren't so bad.

"Um, I think Juice. You know the movie with Tupac in it?" Yasmine laughs a little. "Um." She looks back at her card. "What's something that scares you?"

What? Why was that question so deep but she got a silly question? I tried to push back my annoyance but could barely hide it. I just shrugged. "I don't know."

That's when Mr. Moore decided to speak. "Not an answer."

He was making this more difficult than he needed it to be.

I let out an annoyed sigh and rolled my shoulders back. "I don't know. Nothing."

"We're going to be stuck on this until you can give a clear answer."

Oh..my..god.

I tried to think really hard. What was I scared of? Not death. Death wasn't scary. The unknown didn't scare me either. Failure didn't even scare me anymore because I've already failed so many times.

So what did?

The image of my mom pops in my head. I try to disregard it but that's all I could see. That's all I can see is my mother.

"Ending up like my mom, I guess." I spoke in almost a whisper.

Mr. Moore seemed good on the answer and motioned for the questions to move forward.

I looked at my card. "Why your favorite fruit and why?" Are you Screwing kidding me? Again with the stupid questions?

Yasmine didn't have to think hard on it. "Apples. I love apples. Especially when they're crispy." She looks back at her card. "What's something you least like about yourself?"

How in the hell was I getting all the personal questions? I sat in my seat, uncomfortable by the question. I wanted to say, "everything" but I didn't want people thinking I was an attention seeker.

I also didn't want to say I "didn't know" because that would just prolong this even further.

"My mind, I guess."

Mr. Moore motioned for Yasmine to say something. She got the hint. "What about your mind?"

Do I really have to elaborate?

"Sometimes I think I'm the worst person on the planet. Like I'm the craptiest person in the world. Sometimes I feel like I can't do anything. Like I'm stuck. I don't want to be stuck. I guess my mind controls that."

I saw all eyes on me. It made me clear my throat and sit up straight in my seat. I go to the next question. "What do you like to do the most?"

Oh, come Screwing on.

Yasmine thinks a little. "Maybe read. I like reading. It helps me relax." She looks back at her questions. "Are you a good person?"

I was done. I had it to my limit. I didn't want to be a part of this anymore and if they wanted to kick me out of the school then so be it.

I grabbed my things. "I'm done. This is stupid." And walked my ass straight out the door.

'You're a crapty person. You'll always be a crapty person. Look at you. You can't even handle a few questions.'

My thoughts raced. So much so that it gave me a literal headache.

Why was I getting all the personal questions? I didn't understand it. Why was I the only one getting targeted? I hated this. I hated him.

"Amara?!" Mr. Moore shouted after me.

I rolled my eyes and stopped at the end of the hallway so he could catch up to me. "If this is the part where you write me up then go ahead because I don't care. This whole thing is stupid. Why am I the only one getting asked questions like that? Then everyone is sitting in that room, judging me on everything I do and it's not fair."

Mr. Moore didn't seem upset by my outburst in anger. Instead, he just spoke calmly. "You want to know why I gave

you those questions?" I nodded. "It was a test and you failed."
I looked at him confused. "Amara, I know you think my class
is a waste of time and I did that to show you just how quick
you can get mad. That's why you need this class. You couldn't
handle Yasmine asking you five questions without getting
upset. In the real world, you can't do that."

Knowing that Mr. Moore wasn't just out to get me made
my temper be put to rest. I even felt embarrassed at my
outburst. I go to my nails and start picking at them. "I don't
know if I can do this."

Mr. Moore pauses a little. Probably trying to find the
right words before he spoke them out to existence. "A couple
days ago, you told me you didn't know your worth. Why are
you here at this school Amara?"

I think about it a little. I still don't look at him. "Because
I want to be better. I want to be a better person."

"Because you think you deserve it? See, somewhere down there, you know you are worth more than what you let on and one day you'll get to it and I don't mind helping along the way. Right now though, you need to go back in the classroom and finish your questions because in my class, we don't quit."

I was so used to quitting that the motto he had shocked me. I couldn't quit? Then I realized that quitting was easy. That's why I liked to quit.

No more quitting.

Chapter Eleven
BUTTERFLIES

THREE MONTHS LATER

I can't believe it's been three months and I'm 50% in my trade. I didn't think I could do it. Turns out I could do it. I just put in the work. Hard work really paid off in the long run.

The two people I had to really thank were Zaria and Zane. They've been my rock throughout the entire time. Them and Ms. Ranoni have been here to help me through thick and thin.

I just took what everyone has been telling me and what I've been telling myself. That I need to focus on the positive. Just focus on the positive and everything will be fine.

I've been so productive for some reason. I've been doing so well and it's scaring me. How the hell did I just flip a switch like this?

I want to question it a little but I also don't. I just need to power through with it. Just focus on the positives.

Focus on the positives Amara.

The Sneaker Ball was coming up. I wasn't planning on going. I was just going to sit in my dorm room and count the minutes that went by.

I was at my lunch table, eating when Zane walked up to the table. "Hey, Amara." He sits down next to me.

"Hey, Zane." I noticed the look he had on his face. He looked nervous. Scared even. "Are you okay? You don't look too good."

Zane nodded back with confidence. "Yeah, I'm fine." He cleared his throat. He unzips his backpack and pulls something out. It's a bouquet of roses. "These are for you?"

Roses? For me? This couldn't be what I thought it was...could it?

To be honest I always found Zane attractive. That and the way he was so good at comforting me always gave me butterflies. He was so good to me but I thought it would never happen.

'Know your worth, Amara.'

"Me? Why?" I questioned instead of disregarding like I would normally do.

"I was wondering if you wanted to go to The Sneaker Ball with me?"

'Is this actually happening? Amara keep cool. Keep it cool.'

I wanted to say, "why me?" Out of an old habit of me putting myself down. I realized I had to stop putting myself down. Not only was it bad for my mental health, it wasn't a good look on me.

I had to just stay positive and for some reason I felt way more positive today.

"Great!"

Zane seemed surprised at me accepting this. It kind of made me feel bad about myself. Was all I known for was negativity? Was that all I was ever going to be known for?

"Cool." Zane stands up from his seat. "I'll see you Friday then?"

"Yeah. I'll see you."

Then I realized I don't even have a dress to go to The Sneaker Ball. I mentally cursed at myself. I was definitely going to need Zaria's help.

I felt someone tap my shoulder. When I turned around I saw it was Hannah. I couldn't help but roll my eyes as I turned back around to continue eating my lunch. "What do you want?"

Hannah sits down next to me. "Listen, I wanted to say I'm sorry for everything I did. It was really immature of me and...I shouldn't have treated you like that."

I was actually shocked. Hannah of all people apologizing to me? It was unreal to me. Maybe it was my new attitude that was drawing people in.

I didn't want any problems to be honest so I just nodded. "Right. Okay, thanks."

Hannah looks at my food. She notices I scraped the mustard off my chili dog. "No mustard?"

"I hate it."

All she does is nod. "Well, see you at The Sneaker Ball." She gets out of her seat. "Hope you and Zane win, the Sneaker king and queen!" She winks at me. Then walks away.

I found that odd but didn't say anything.

I really gotta tell Zaria about my day.

Chapter Twelve
WASTE OF SPACE

Telling Zaria everything that happened was a trip for sure. She wanted all the details. Was saying that she had been waiting for this day to finally come. I told her she sounded stupid.

The thought of Zane asking me out still invades my mind. I wanted to question everything about it. Why me? Why would he ever want to ask out a girl like me but I try to push those thoughts away. I had to be positive. I needed to be more positive.

I didn't even know what to wear as a dress. It wouldn't look good on me. Not in a long shot but Zaria insisted I would wear one.

Whatever it was it better have not been the color green.

I tried on the red dress she gave me. I looked in the mirror. It was sparkly. It looked like diamonds. Small spaghetti straps hung on my shoulders. It looked amazing I had to admit.

I didn't want to give her the satisfaction she actually found a dress I liked but she did it. I guess that was the magic behind Zaria. She could always make you look good.

I walked out the dressing room and Zaria gasped at my dress. "Oh my god. Zane is going to be all over you."

I rolled my eyes slightly. "Please."

"You'll have fun. Trust me." Zaria looked over to Hannah and Ashanti laughing together. She grumbled. "I can't stand them."

I shrugged. "Hannah apologized to me earlier."

Zaria gave me a look like she couldn't believe it. "Really?" She looked back at them. "Do you feel it was sincere?"

"Maybe." I say. "She probably wants to put the whole thing behind her."

Zaria thought about it. "It's just kinda weird. You would think she would be all over this considering everyone knows now that Zane is taking you to The Sneaker Ball."

I sighed loudly at it. "Why does everyone already know?"

"Girl are you serious? You're both on the ballet for Sneaker King and Queen."

This could not be happening.

I rubbed my eyes in frustration. "Oh my god! I didn't want this to happen."

"This is a good thing! If you win, you'll be hot and popular."

"I don't want to be 'hot and popular!' I like my bubble. It;s a pretty nice bubble."

"You'll be fine. Trust me."

Trusting Zaria? Mind as well kill me at this point.

Chapter Thirteen
END OF THE LINE

Zane told me to wait for him outside of the Rec. I looked at my phone, counting down the minutes of when he would get here.

He wanted to at least know what color dress I was wearing so we could match. I told him the color so he should be wearing a red tux or something like red.

I had to admit, I was nervous. I never really done this before. At my old school I never got to do stuff like this. My anxiety would always prevent me. I would always miss out.

Maybe Zaria was right. Maybe this would be good for me. Hopefully it will be good for me.

Zane walks over to me. His mouth dropped to the floor. I feel like he's being a little over dramatic but I let it slide.

I don't know why I feel this sudden irritation coming from me. It's not something I can control either. I feel lost with the feeling. I don't want to ruin this evening with Zane so I'll just bury it deep.

"You look beautiful."

Had to believe in myself. I did look pretty in this dress with my red sneakers. He was right.

"Can we go talk for a second?" I asked him.

Zane nodded. "Of course."

I take Zane's hand and walk him all the way over to the basketball court. We sat down.

"I'm just nervous about tonight."

"Yeah, I didn't expect them to put our names for Sneaker King and Queen. I would've warned you sooner if I had known."

"It's okay, I should've known better. You're the popular guy. Of course it would happen." Zane chuckles at the title he holds. I sigh a little. "Sorry, today has just been a tough day for me."

Zane nodded. "Been one for me too."

I looked at him, curiously. "What's wrong with you?"

Zane looks away from me. He starts pressing on his knuckles. Probably a form of anxiety. I quickly grabbed his hand to stop him. He looks at me and smiles before speaking. "Today is a year from when my daughter died."

I didn't even know Zane had a daughter. He probably didn't feel comfortable enough with telling me beforehand. "Oh my god. I'm so sorry."

"It's okay. You're not the one that killed her."

The statement kind of shook me to my core. "Someone killed her?"

I think he felt comfortable telling me his story. "My baby mama and I weren't always on the same page. I always thought she was a liar. So, one night when she had our daughter with her, she claimed someone was breaking in. I thought it was some pathetic attempt at getting me to come back to the house. Come to find out...it was a robber. He ended up killing both her and my child...they still haven't found the guy who did it."

He shakes his head, anger consuming him. "There was hardly anything to take. She was barely making ends meet. That's why I was doing stuff on the streets. To support my daughter. He could've just taken whatever was out. He didn't have to kill them...he didn't have to kill her."

I rested my hand on his shoulder. "You know it's not your fault right? None of that is your fault."

"I know but I...I still feel like somehow I'm responsible. If I had just believed her for a second then maybe things would have ended differently."

Zane looks into the sky. "Do you believe in God?"

I shake my head. "Not particularly, no."

"I believe that my daughter is up there, playing with her little cars. She was only one. How could he do this?"

I didn't know what else to say. I was bad at these things. I couldn't even comfort myself. How was I supposed to comfort another person?

Zane shook his head at me. "You don't have to say anything. Just you listening means the world to me."

I smile at him. We hear footsteps behind us. It's Hannah. "Come on, guys. They're about to announce who's the Sneaker Queen and King."

I raised a brow at this. Why was she so eager for us to come in? It was a little suspicious. I see her walk over and talk to Ashanti.

I had to figure out this mess. I look over to Zane. "Go in there, I'll follow you after."

"Alright." He kisses my cheek and stands up before walking away from me.

I go towards Ashanti and Hannah. I make sure my footsteps are low. I don't want to be heard or seen.

I get to them. I make sure to keep my distance while listening in. "I don't know Hannah. It sounds kind of mean."

"She stole Zane from me! She's not getting away with it. We're going to be behind the stage and once they put the crown on her we're going to dump a bucket of mustard on her and you can't back out."

Are you kidding me? This was straight out of a horror movie I swear to God. She wasn't going to get away with this. Not even in the slightest.

I walk into the Rec. I see Zane standing by the snacks. I walk over to him. He notices the angry expression on my face. "What's up?"

"You'll see." I simply say.

"Alright, can I have everyone's attention?" Ms. McCann says. "Hope you all been havin' the time of your life. We gotta get down to who the Sneaker King and Queen is so let's get to it."

They all cheer. I just wanted this to hurry up so I can do what I needed to do. She opens up an envelope. "Your Sneaker King is Zane Graham!"

Everyone cheers. Especially the boys. They all exchange handshakes. Zane kisses me on the forehead. "I'll see you up there."

I simply nod to him with a fake smile. He walks over to stand on the stage.

"And your Sneaker Queen is..." She opens the other envelope. "Amara Jones!"

Not that many people cheered for me as much as Zane but they still cheered. I put on my fake smile and waved at everyone before going up on stage.

I stood there. One of the girls put the sash on me and was about to put the crown on me. I stopped her. "Wait." She gives me a confused look. I take the microphone from Ms.

McCann and step up so everybody can see me. "I just wanted to say...thank you to all the votes but I don't deserve this award. I mean I think most of us can agree on that."

"What are you doing?" Zane whispered to me.

"Giving the people what they want. You all don't like me. Mind as well not fake it. I just believe one girl truly deserves this whole thing. Let's give it up for Hannah Riley!"

Everyone is confused but claps anyway. Hannah comes from backstage also confused. "Amara, what are you doing?"

"Don't act dumb. I'm giving you what you want. You want to be Sneaker Queen with Zane, be my guest. Don't let me stop you."

I took the crown from the girl and placed it on Hannah's head. "You see guys, Hannah is a lot of things: pretty, smart, athletic."

Hannah smiles at the compliments thinking they're sincere. "Thank you, Amara."

I start to walk backstage. "She's also a two faced, lying, manipulative girl that will put herself over anyone else."

Everyone gasps at what I said. "Ms. Jones, enough!" Ms. McCann tells me.

"Oh trust me, I'm over it." I told her. I walk backstage and push Ashanti to the ground letting whatever she was holding go.

The bucket of Mustard dropped all over Hannah and her green dress. Some even got on Zane. I laugh at this. She finally got what she deserved. After all this time.

Knowing I was going to be in big trouble, I walked out of the Rec. I hear footsteps following me. "What are you doing?! Do you know what's going to happen to you?"

It was Zane. I ignored him and kept walking. "She was going to do it to me, Zane. I just beat her to it."

"Yeah, well it didn't look that way to Ms. McCann and Mr. Cleaves. You're not getting out of this."

I finally turned to him. "What if I don't want to get out of this. I hate it here. I hate the people here. I just...I want to disappear."

He gives me a confused glance. "You're literally almost done with your trade. Why are you throwing it all away?"

"Because too much is wrong with me! That's the problem isn't it?" I question him.

Zane shakes his head. "I never said that."

"You didn't have to. You think I want to go to these lame after school events with you? I don't want to do any of this. This isn't what I signed for. I hate this school." I didn't realize that tears were slipping down my face. "I hate this school. I hate this place!" I then felt my chest tighten. "What's happening to me?"

Zane looked at me full of concern. "What's wrong? Amara what's wrong?"

"I can't breathe. I can't breathe. I can't..." I fall down to my knees and clutch my chest. I start to sob hard. "I can't breathe!"

"Whoa, hey, hey." He bends down to my level. "You're having a panic attack. It's okay. Breathe."

He hugs me. I just sob in his arms. "I don't want to do this anymore." I sobbed loudly.

Mr. Cleaves had reached us. He didn't expect to see me fall apart I guess. "Amara, are you okay?"

"No...I'm not..." I said truthfully. "I just want everything to stop."

Why can't anything just stop?

Chapter Fourteen
LIKE MOTHER, LIKE DAUGHTER

"So you have just been diagnosed with Bipolar Two. How does it feel?" My therapist, Mr. Whitmore asked me.

I didn't want to answer. I didn't want to feel. I didn't want to do any of it. I'm not Screwing Bipolar. I am not like my mother. I will not have these Screwing lunatics describe me to be a monster.

I AM NOT A MONSTER.

My mom? Could win an award for doing her monstrous things. Woman blamed her suicide on me. Me? I would never do something like that. This whole thing was stupid.

"I'm not Bipolar." I say, not looking at him.

Mr. Whitmore pauses. Probably trying to choose his words carefully. What am I? Fragile?

"Do you believe that you reject your diagnosis because it is the same as your mothers'?"

To that, I look at him with pure hatred. How dare he bring up my mother. I didn't even want to do this to begin with but the school wouldn't let me come back until I got some help.

This was their so-called "help."

I wanted to scream at him. Kick my feet and yell but that would just make everything worse. They already think I'm the crazy girl with a dead mom. So, I won't show them that side of me. I'll bury it deep inside of me.

I don't say anything. I want him to know that I hate this. I wanted to make him feel uncomfortable. I don't think it was working. Maybe he was used to his "patients" acting like this.

So, I decided to speak. "What does my mother have anything to do with this?"

"Well, some patients seem to develop a sort of...guilt when they notice they have similarities to their parents."

I shook my head. "I am nothing like her." I couldn't believe he would even say that. "I didn't kill myself over someone leaving me. I dumped Mustard on a girl at my school. Those don't compare."

Mr. Whitmore nodded at my words but I don't think he truly got it. He was just trying to acknowledge my words. "Bipolar is a genetic and environmental mental illness. It's not your fault."

It being not my fault set me at ease a little. I leaned back in my seat and let him continue to talk.

"Bipolar can cause poor decision making, depression, losing interest in things, racing thoughts, feeling worthless, the list goes on."

'Why does it sound like me? No. No it's not me. It can't be me. It will never be me.'

"Sorry to tell you doc, but that's not me." I told him.

Mr. Whitmore seemed disappointed in my answer. He looks at the time. "I'm afraid that's all the time we have left-"

I didn't even let him finish his sentence. I ran out the room. In the waiting room, I see a mother on the phone with someone. Her kid was running around, screaming.

She seemed too preoccupied. I don't know if I want to be a mother. It's not about even if I want to, it's about if I'm able to. I don't think I have it in me.

I noticed something in her purse. It was a bottle of pills.

I play it off, walking over and grabbing a magazine. There on the pills it said they were xanax. The same pills Wyatt gave me to get me to sleep with him.

I remember the relaxing feeling. It was calming to me. Everything about the world stopped. I was able to breathe normally. To just simply exist.

I made sure she wasn't looking and grabbed the bottle of pills before walking out the office.

I leaned against the brick wall and put one pill in my hand. I stared at it for a moment. Then I put it in my mouth and swallowed it.

Maybe I'll regret it later but hey, you only live once right?

Chapter Fifteen
RAGE WILL FILL YOUR SOUL

Being back at my dorm was weird. They switched Hannah out of my room and put her in somebody else's. Ashanti was barely in the room. Probably because of her friendship with Hannah. It was just me and Zaria. Except Zaria wasn't here.

I felt drowsy. It was a calming sensation that ran through my body. I even felt a little sleepy. Hell, I think I am sleeping right now and I don't know how to wake myself back up.

I don't know why but I loved it.

I giggled to myself a little. Everything seemed right. Everything was going to go right. I had to tell myself that.

It was a blissful high. A high that felt so right and a high that would be kept to myself.

If I could control it that is.

I heard someone open the door. There was Zaria. I think I was zoning out a little.

I saw Zane right behind her at the door. I wave a little, giggling. "Hello, Zany!" I laughed at what I said and fell back on my bed.

Zane and Zaria gave each other a look. Zane looked around to see if anyone was watching and mumbled, "Screw it," before walking into my room and closing the door behind him.

"Ooh." I say. "Zane walked in the girl's room. He's gonna get in trouble."

Zane walked straight up to me. He grabbed my chin, making me look in his eyes. When he realized I couldn't even hold eye contact and started to fall asleep on him, he removed his hand. "Are you high right now?"

"I don't know mom." I tilt my head at him. "Am I?"

Zaria rubbed her temples in frustration. "Jesus Christ, Amara. Do you know what will happen to you if this gets out?"

"It won't get out because you guys aren't going to say anything."

Zane stared at me in pure disappointment. I don't know why it made me feel bad but it did. He shook his head and went straight for my closet. "Where is it?"

When I noticed he was going through my things, I ran over to him. "Don't touch my stuff!"

"Where is it?!"

"Don't touch anything!"

"Where are the pills, Amara?"

"I SAID DON'T TOUCH ANYTHING!" I smacked Zane right across the face.

I was shocked at what I did. Zaria seemed to be too because she had her hand over her mouth.

Zane touched his cheek a little, startled at what I did. He tried to have no reaction but he was hurt. He was hurt at what I did. "What the hell is wrong with you?"

I try to defend myself. "What the hell is wrong with me? What the hell is wrong with you? Going through my stuff like you own the place."

"I'm doing this because I care about you."

"Oh my god. Enough of the heroics. You don't give a crap about me because you don't Screwing have to."

"I-" Zaria tries to speak.

I held up my hand to her. "Stay out of this, Zaria." I turn to walk away but Zane grabs my arm and keeps me in place.

"You're right. I don't have to give a crap about you but I do. You know I do. Are you blind? Can't you see the way I feel about you? And you're going to do this? What are you some kind of addict?!"

The thought of being compared to an addict affected me. More than he realized. I would not be called the same nickname as my dead mother.

"I am *not* an addict. You don't know anything."

"I know that whatever you're taking is going to affect your Bipolar meds so I'm going to need you to get it together."

At that, I laughed. I clapped my hands together. "Well, big twist of the century there Zane because I'm not taking my meds."

Zane gave me a look. "You know if you don't take them, you can't stay here. They see you as a threat."

"No, they see me as some mentally ill lunatic and I will not be known as the girl with Bipolar. No thank you."

"So what? I'm just supposed to sit here and watch you destroy yourself!"

I crossed my arms at him. I was going to say something that was messed up but it was the only way to get him to back off. "You know you keep trying to take care of people but you really suck at that. I mean, isn't that why your daughter died?"

Silence. Complete silence. He looked at me in shock that I would even say that.

Zaria shook her head at me. "Amara-"

"No, Zaria. Let me continue. Or does our hero want to give a speech on how he can save me and blah blah blah." I made sure to get right in his face as I spoke. "Go cry to your daughter's grave instead of saving someone that doesn't need to be saved."

That got him. I knew it did. "Screw you."

I laughed. I backed away a little and wiped some of the tears that were coming down my face. "Oh? There he is! The big bad Zane that everyone is so afraid of. What are you gonna do? Hit me? Hit me, Zane. I bet it would make you feel better."

He doesn't reply back. He just points at me. "You and me, we're done."

"Come on, Zane." Zaria said. "You don't mean that."

"Oh I mean every word." He looks back at me. "You are dead to me. You want to end up like your mother then go ahead. I can't stop you. Be the very thing you're afraid to become because I am done being your friend and I am done loving you."

He loved me? Zane loved me?

Zane walks out the room and I stand there in shock at his confession.

Zaria walks in front of me. "You really messed up, A." She says to me before grabbing her things and walking out.

Did I really mess everything up?

Chapter Sixteen
BREAK YOU

This was probably the dumbest thing I could have possibly done. I decided to text my dad to see to meet up with me finally. I don't know why I did it. Maybe it was because he was the only person I had left.

I wait at the coffee shop. I pick at my nails, anxiety taking over me. Maybe this was a mistake. Maybe I shouldn't have done this.

I took out some xanax and looked at them. I didn't have the heart to take them. All I could do was stare at them.

"Are you on some medication, Bridgette?"

I looked up to see my dad. I quickly put the pills away and went back to picking at my nails. "Don't call me by my middle name."

He tilts his head at me. He notices me picking at my skin. "Your mother used to do that."

"Yeah, because she was a crackhead." I realized the irony that he would never get and decided to just shut up.

My dad sits down across from me. He rests his hands on the table. "How's school been coming along?"

I shrugged. "Almost got kicked out because I dumped mustard on this girl."

He didn't seem surprised. Was I really that much of an angry person? "I'm assuming she deserved it?"

"More than you know."

There was silence. He clears his throat slightly. "Thank you for seeing me but why after all this time have you?"

I decided just to tell him. I also wanted to see his reaction to when I did tell him. "I got diagnosed with Bipolar Two."

He pauses. He definitely wasn't expecting that. How else would I break the news that his daughter is a lunatic? "How does that make you feel?"

"Stupid. I feel stupid."

"It's not your fault."

"If you don't care that I have it, why did you leave mom?"

Dad sighs but he had to have known this day would come. "I couldn't deal with it anymore. She would hit me. Abuse me. She couldn't stay off the drugs. I just couldn't do it." He stops me from picking at my nails. "But that isn't your fault. And I'm sorry. I know that doesn't excuse anything. I should've been there for you. Instead I was a coward but I want to make it right."

I don't know if I could give my dad a second chance. Him leaving really messed me up. I had no one to protect me. I had nothing.

Something inside of me figured he changed. I don't know why or how but I could feel it.

"Okay." I said to him, "But we can't move too fast. I don't think I'm ready for all that father daughter crap."

My dad nods, excited. "Yes. Absolutely. On your time."

"Great. It's a Sunday. I need to get back to school." I start to stand up from where I've been sitting.

"Do you need a ride?"

"No, I'm good. I like walking. It's calming to me. I'll see you when I see you." I tell him before walking out the door.

When I did, I took out the xanax again. I stared at them. I still didn't have the heart to take them.

I threw the pills somewhere in the distance. I then grabbed my Bipolar medication and took one before swallowing it.

Hope it works.

I don't pray but I do pray that it works.

Chapter Seventeen
HUMAN BEINGS ARE NOT MACHINES

Called down to Mr. Attieh's office. What did I possibly do this time?

Maybe this was it for me. I was done for. Of course I would be done for when I'm actually doing what I'm supposed to be doing and taking my medication.

Mr. Attieh was a pretty nice guy and head of academics so whatever he was calling me in had to do with my grades. Probably so, I did have a 2.8 GPA in high school diploma.

I walk in his office and sit down. "What did I do this time?"

"Nothing, I hope." He laughs a little. "A student was just a little bit worried with you so I wanted to check on you."

Somebody was worried about me? Who? "Really?"

"Yeah." He could see the curiosity on my face. "I can see you want to know. It was Zane. He wanted to make sure you were okay."

Wow. Zane still cared about me? After all I said to him? After everything I've done? "Well, tell him I'm doing better and...I'm going to be okay."

"Are you sure? You've been making sure you're doing the right thing? Remember one more negative incident and you might have to leave the program."

I understood where Mr. Attieh was coming from. He was just doing his job. That's all the instructors here ever do. I finally had to come to terms that they weren't all out to get me.

It was just my mind battling myself. "I understand and I know. I have been doing well. I actually just completed my trade."

Mr. Attieh looks shocked. "What? Congratulations!"

"Thank you. It was hard but I finally did it. Now, I just got to focus on high school and I'll be good to go."

"Just remember to stay focused. Don't let anyone distract you and don't let you distract yourself."

I took in his words and nodded. "I don't think that will happen. I'm determined."

I can do this.

Chapter Eighteen
THE STARS IN OUR LIFE

Becoming a better person was hard. Especially if you are used to your self destructive patterns. It feels hopeless sometimes. Being a better version of yourself. The better you, you yourself want to be.

I knew I could do it. All I needed was a little bit of hope and I got it. That drove me to the edge.

I sat in the circle where everyone was at. I was at a support group for drug addicts. I guess it was my turn to share.

I was a little nervous. I didn't like this. All the attention on me. It was only fair though that I went.

I sighed a little, trying to gather up my thoughts. "Hi, my name is Amara and I'm a drug addict." They all say my name as a form of a greeting and hence the sharing begins.

"All my life, I've been surrounded by drugs. My mother was a drug addict and alcoholic. She abused me, used me, and did anything she could to me to be honest. My dad wasn't around much. He couldn't stand her."

"The first time I took pills was at a party. I wanted to blend in. I didn't want to feel different. So, I took them. The second time I got diagnosed with Bipolar and just...I don't know. I guess I couldn't handle it. Being compared to my mother. It's probably the worst feeling in the world. Knowing you're a crapty person. But I acknowledge that I am a crapty person. So it's got to make me less crapty than all the other crapty people...right?"

Wendy, our support leader, smiles at me. "Thank you for sharing, Amara. It really means a lot."

I nod at her. In the distance behind her, I see someone walk in. I look at them. It's Zane.

I can't believe he's here. After everything I've done to him.

"Excuse me for a moment." I say before walking over to Zane. "Hey, what are you doing here?"

"I got one of the ladies in Wellness to crack. She said you would be here."

I knew right at this moment I had to apologize. "Look I-" We both talk at the same time.

"Let me go first." I told him. "Listen, what I did to you was really messed up. I don't know how I can put it into words that I'm sorry. I'm so sorry, Zane. I don't know. I guess my psychiatrist told me it was an episode and it's not an excuse at all for what I did, it's just...I don't know. I don't want to say something and for you to think I'm trying to defend myself."

Zane shook his head and waved for me to continue. "No, no. You're fine. Go ahead."

I paused for a moment to gather my thoughts. "I don't know how to do this. This whole 'love' thing because I never got it. I mean I know you're almost right there with me in that department but I...my brain just works so stupid sometimes. And most of the time, as long as I'm taking my meds, I'll be fine."

"But then there are those bad times. The dark days. And those days I'm not gonna be fine. I'm gonna be all over the place, mad at the entire world, throwing the biggest fit. Or I might just not be able to get out of bed at all just from my depression. And if you can't handle what comes from...from being with someone with Bipolar then maybe we shouldn't do this."

Zane listened to me carefully. He took everything I said in. "I'm sorry too. You were going through a rough time and I pushed you away. I should have never pushed you away. No matter how hard it got because the truth is...I love you, Amara and I don't want you to ever think I'll give up on you. I just thought that maybe if I said that to you, you would get your act together. I never meant..I never meant to hurt you like that."

He takes my hands in his. "I'm ready for anything. Believe that. You can throw the whole world at me and I won't back down. Not ever."

I never had someone be so sweet to me. It made me smile. I stood on my tippy toes and kissed him.

It was like magic. Everything was going to be okay.

Chapter Nineteen
THE BEAUTY IN YOURSELF

Dear Mr. Martin,

I just wanted to say that you were right to kick me out of your classroom. I know how hard it was for you to do. Probably one of the hardest things you had to do to a student but I get it though. I had to see my flaws and my wrongs.

The truth is I've been doing horrible things since my departure from high school. I got into this program with the help of Ms. Preston. It's called Detroit Job Corp. The place isn't really so bad. It's more so myself. I had to deal with my own issues.

It's been really tough but I want you to know that I'm doing better. I'm gonna make it and get through it. I also want you to know that everything I do is not your fault. You are not the reason why I am like this. You shouldn't feel guilty.

Thank you for being one of the first people to open my eyes to my madness and also thank you for still being my favorite teacher after everything I've been through.

Sincerely, Amara Jones.

Chapter Twenty
HAPPINESS

SIX MONTHS LATER

I don't know how I did it but I did it. I'm done with every Screwing thing.

I've never been so excited for myself before. Being on this stage means everything to me. My biggest accomplishment of all. Battling myself.

When you battle yourself it's exhausting. It's a never ending cycle of just doubting yourself all of the time. Feeling like you can't be the best.

I am now finally rewarded. I wait for them to call my name. "Amara Jones." I hear Ms. Stephens say. I happily walk across the stage and give her a hug.

Ms. Stephens hugs me back. I shake hands with Mr. Hanes and walk across the stage. I sit down with the rest of the students. I see Zane blow a kiss at me and I blew one back.

My dad gives me a thumbs up. I give one back to him with a smile.

When graduation is over, I walk over to my boyfriend and my father. Zane gives me a bunch of roses to which I kiss him on the cheek as a thank you.

My dad just smiles at me. "You know I'm proud of you right?"

I never was told people were proud of me growing up. There wasn't anyone to tell me they were proud of me. It meant something to me. So much more than he realized.

He could have disappeared forever and yeah, I still hate him for what he did but now I understand. We had an understanding. I went up and hugged him, tears in my eyes, I said, "I'm proud of you too."

I'm the reason I did all of this. Nobody else. I did it all by myself and I'm glad. I'm glad I actually made something out of myself. I feel like I can do almost anything. Like I'm on top of the world but not because of a "hypomanic" episode. Like I can actually do it.

And that is the best feeling in the world.

I imagine the life I will have with Zane in the future. Married with three kids. Hopefully two girls and one boy. I want a big house. Something to help fill the hole in my heart of not having a family growing up. I want family dinners, Christmas gatherings, and decorating our house. Being with each other. Forever.

I imagine my dad as this grandpa that spoils his grandchildren to bits and pieces. He loves them with everything. He'll try to make up for the past mistakes he has made.

I'll smile to myself. My boyfriend will wrap his arms around me as we watch the three children, Zane Jr, Zaria-Anne, and Bridgette play around the living room. My father chased them around the house as if they were playing tag.

Happiness. Just utter Happiness.

The end.

Even though Amara is not a real person, there are a lot of
people that can relate to her struggle. You are not alone.
Accomplish your goals, see the light. If nobody told you they
believed in you, just know that I believe in you!